NOBODY'S GIRL

PATRICIA HERMES

A YEARLING BOOK

Published by
Dell Publishing Co., Inc.
1 Dag Hammarskjold Plaza
New York, New York 10017

Yearling ® TM 913705, Dell Publishing Co., Inc.

ISBN: 0-440-46523-0

Reprinted by arrangement with Harcourt Brace Jovanovich, Inc.
Printed in the United States of America

February 1983

10 9 8 7 6

CW

*For Barbara Lucas,
my editor, and teacher, and friend.
And especially for my children,
Matthew and Jennifer,
whose book this really is*

NOBODY'S FAULT?

1

Someday. I knew I was going to do it. I would be the first woman in the major leagues. I could see it now, my name in "Sports Monday": "Emily Taylor bats .500; fifth consecutive year."

I picked up the ball from the grass and threw it hard against the garage wall. It rolled back to me easily, and I crouched down, my glove on the ground in front of me, just the way my brother, Monse, tells me, when he plays with me at all. *Body in front of the ball, eye on the ball.* Now if I would just stop being scared of it, I knew I'd make the big leagues. I was picturing my name in the headlines when the ball went past me . . . right between my legs.

"Nice catch!" Somebody laughed.

I whirled around. It was Monse, perched on his

bike, grinning that stupid grin he has when he teases me. He was wearing his blue baseball shirt and hat that he wears all the time so everybody will know he's on a team.

"Nice catch!" he said again.

I made a face at him, then turned back and threw the ball against the wall really hard. I'd show him! Only this time it didn't roll, but bounced high, right at my head. I ducked and closed my eyes, and it zinged over me.

Monse laughed again. "Nice—catch—Emily!"

I spun around. "Shut up, Monse!" I shouted. "Just go away!"

Monse was still laughing as he started to pedal away on his bike. "You'll never make it in the majors," he called over his shoulder. "You throw just like a girl."

I don't think I really meant to do it. I *know* I didn't think I could hit him, but I threw my glove at him. Somehow I did hit him—right in the back of the head.

Monse stopped and jumped off his bike. I think he was as surprised as I was that I could aim that well. He was mad, too. "That's not funny, Emily," he said, starting after me.

I turned and ran into the house, stopping in the kitchen to listen. Monse must have thought I was in my room because he came in the side door and was starting up the front stairs. I practically flew up the back ones. The back stairs are closest to my room, and I got there before he did. I ran into the room and slammed the door, leaning back against it to hold it closed.

I knew he could open it, even with me leaning against it, so I looked around for something to help. It was then I realized that it was awfully quiet out there. I couldn't hear Monse breathing hard or laughing the way he always does when he's teasing me. Maybe Millie had stopped him when he was running upstairs. Millie's our housekeeper, and she's been taking care of us for about a million years because Mom and Daddy both work. But I hadn't heard her come in and tell him to stop, so he must still be there. He'd never give up that fast.

I pressed my ear against the door, listening. Still no sound out there, not even any breathing. Keeping my foot against the door, very quietly I opened it a crack.

"Yah! Got you!" Monse yelled. He pushed the door hard, and it flew open, right into my face.

"Oww! Oww! My nose!"

"Serves you right! That's what you get for— Oh, wow! Oh, Emily, I'm sorry! I didn't mean to *hurt* you." Monse was staring at me, wide-eyed. He reached into the pocket of his jeans and pulled something out, a rag or a scarf. Maybe it used to be a handkerchief, but it was gray. "Here, use this."

"I don't want it!" I pushed it away. My nose hurt a lot, and I wiped it with my hand. That's when I saw it. *Blood*! Oh, no, blood! I pushed past Monse and ran down the back stairs. "Millie!" I shouted. "Oh, Millie, I'm dead!"

I could hear Monse running after me. "Emily, wait!"

I was in the kitchen, but there was no Millie, and I collapsed on the back steps, crying.

Monse ran around me, then stood in front of me, blocking my way to the kitchen. "Emily, I'm sorry," he said really softly. "Look, I didn't mean to hurt you, you know that. Please shush."

I knew why he wanted me to shush, so Millie wouldn't hear. Millie thinks Monse is wonderful, and every time he teases me, she says it's all my fault, but Monse knew she couldn't help seeing it wasn't my fault this time. I stopped screaming, even though I was still crying. It was because of the blood. I'm just scared of it. Well, maybe not scared but worried.

I looked up at Monse. He knows how I am about blood, and I was afraid he'd split his sides laughing if I said this, but I had to say it anyway. "Am I going to bleed to death?" I asked.

He didn't laugh, but he did make a face at me. "People don't bleed to death, dummy," he said. "It's just a regular bloody nose. Now listen, if you stop crying I'll give you something. I have some neat stuff in my room." He held out his handkerchief again, and this time I took it and held it against my nose.

"Like whad?" I said, my voice coming out sort of funny.

"Come look," he answered.

"Okay." I got up off the steps and followed him upstairs. My room is at the top of the stairs on the second floor, and his is at the top on the third floor. He has all sorts of good things in his room, but he never lets me in there. Maybe he had something I wanted, maybe even some good baseball things. When we got to his room, he closed the door, then went over to his bed and started pulling stuff out from under. I watched, pressing the handkerchief against my nose. After a minute I took the handkerchief away and touched my nose gently, testing. I wasn't bleeding anymore, and I took a deep breath of relief.

"Okay," Monse said, handing me something. "How about this?"

It was a diving mask, one of those things you wear underwater in the pool. I've always wanted one, but they cost too much. I took it and looked through, then handed it back. "Forget it!" I said. The glass front was so scratched up I couldn't see anything, not even Monse, who was standing about two inches away from me.

He handed me a baseball then, but even though I was dying for a new ball, I didn't want this one. The cover was half off, and the stuffing was coming out, and I handed that back, too. "I thought you said you had something good," I said.

"It *is* good!" Monse answered, sounding annoyed. He gets like that sometimes—he's all right with me for a while, and then he gets mad. I figured

I'd better not push my luck or I might not get anything. I looked around quickly. There were some neat-looking things on his bedside table.

"What's that?" I asked, pointing to a black box on his table.

"Just a box." Monse shrugged and looked away, so I knew right away that he didn't want to talk about it, and that made me even more curious.

I went over and picked it up then. It didn't look like a box at all, because a box would open. This was more like a cube, with no opening at all. "Come on, tell me," I said. "What is it?"

"A box, I told you!" Monse came over and grabbed it out of my hands. From the way he was looking at me, I knew he couldn't help showing it off. "Here," he said. "Watch."

He held it in his left hand, with his fingers around the sides of it. With his right hand, he grabbed the top and bottom of it and pulled. It came apart. It *was* a box—a secret box!—and big enough inside to hold my secret notebook. It might even be big enough to hold Mary Elizabeth's notebook, too.

"Can I have it?" I said.

"No way!" Monse turned and put it back on his bedside table.

"Please?"

"No! No way! I just got it."

"But I need it. Come on, Monse, please?" I was thinking about the notebook. What a hiding place, from Mom or Millie! I'd never have to worry about anybody reading my writing anymore. I put a hand on my nose and then I looked at Monse. "I'll tell," I said.

I swear I didn't do it on purpose, but all of a sudden, right then, my nose started bleeding again.

"Cut it out!" Monse yelled. "You're messing up my rug!" He grabbed the handkerchief out of my hand and stuffed it against my face. We stood there for a while, very close, just looking at each other, Monse looking really funny. I knew what he was trying to figure out—whether it was worth it or not to keep the box and have everybody find out that he'd given me a bloody nose. Finally, he took a deep breath and let it out, slowly. "All right," he said sadly. "You can have it. But if you tell anybody, Mom or Dad or Millie or anybody, I swear I'll take it back."

"Oh, thanks, Monse! Thanks a lot. I won't tell, I promise."

Monse nodded, still holding the handkerchief against my face, still looking sad. I began to feel sorry for him. I almost started to tell him that, that I didn't want his old box, that he could keep it himself if he really wanted to. But then he made a face at me, and he stuck the box in my hands. "Get out of here," he said. "Take your drippy nose somewhere else."

"I'm going!"

I held the box tight against my chest with one hand and the handkerchief against my nose with the other. I didn't even care if my nose was bleeding or not, and I ran down the stairs. I just wanted to talk to my friend Mary Elizabeth because now that I had this box, we had something really important to do.

2

I tiptoed down the back stairs to the kitchen, where the phone is, praying that I wouldn't see Millie. She won't let me use the phone to talk to Mary Elizabeth because she says it's a sin to phone somebody who lives practically next door—but I had to talk to Mary Elizabeth right away.

I was trying to dial very quietly when I saw the note from Millie on the blackboard. I guess I had been screaming so much before I hadn't noticed it. "Went grocery shopping," it said. "Be back soon. Be good and *don't fight*. Love, Millie." She had underlined "Don't fight." Millie really knows about Monse and me.

The phone rang in Mary Elizabeth's house, and I could picture her running to answer it. She's been my best friend since we were in first grade, and we know everything about each other. We like the same things, like baseball and the secret notebooks that we write our private thoughts in, and we even hate the same things, like math and mean teachers. But the one thing that's wrong about her lately is that she keeps changing, and I'm never sure what she's going to do next. She's even trying to change her voice, to make it "throaty." She used to have a really nice voice, but now half the time she sounds like a toad.

The phone rang about a million times, and I was just getting ready to hang up when somebody answered. It was either Mary Elizabeth or a frog. "Hello," it croaked.

I didn't answer.

"Hello?"

I still didn't answer, figuring if I waited long enough, she'd get mad and use her regular voice.

"Hello!" she said, finally, good and mad and good and regular.

"Mary Elizabeth!" I said. "Come on over right away and bring your notebook. Wait'll you see what I've got."

"The—notebook?" The way she said it, I could picture her, her nose all wrinkled up as if something smelled bad. "Oh."

"Come on, please? It's something really neat, something new I've got. You'll love it."

"All right," she said slowly. "Okay."

"See you!" I hung up. I knew it would take only a minute for her to get here. We have this long, curvy driveway that winds down past our house and past a little field in the back, and right at the foot of the drive is Mary Elizabeth's house. While I waited, I went into the downstairs bathroom to look at my nose. I leaned over the sink and checked in the mirror, and I could hardly believe it—my nose was fine! It wasn't even red, and it wasn't smushed, but one of my eyes was swollen and getting discolored, as if I were going to have a black eye. How could that happen? Oh, boy, now would Monse and I be in trouble! When Millie saw me, she'd probably start to yell, the way she always does when one of us gets hurt, and Mom would be mad because we were fighting. Crumb!

But then I could tell that Mary Elizabeth was at the back door because the porch shook. She might talk like a frog, but she walks like an elephant. I opened the door.

Mary Elizabeth was carrying her notebook, and she stopped short when she saw me and started to laugh. "What happened to you?"

"Monse . . ." I started to say, but stopped, remembering my promise. "I can't tell you."

Mary Elizabeth's eyebrows shot up. "Huh? Why not? We tell each other everything."

"Yeah, I know, but . . ." I paused, thinking fast, then blurted out, "It's something about Monse, he did something, but he gave me something not to tell and he'll take it back if I do, understand?"

She shrugged. "I guess." But I could tell that she didn't.

I looked at her for a minute, thinking. "All right," I said with a sigh. "I'll tell you. Come on."

I picked up the box from the kitchen counter, and we both ran upstairs and into my room. I closed the door behind us. "Look," I said, holding out the box. "It's a secret box, and I'll show you in a minute how it works." I told her then what had happened and how Monse had given it to me as a bribe so I wouldn't tell.

"You poor kid," Mary Elizabeth said when I finished. "I'd hate to have Monse as a brother. What a pain!"

I shrugged, but I felt just a little bad when she said that. "He's . . . okay," I said. "But listen, you won't tell anybody?"

"Who would I tell? I never talk to Monse anyway."

"Okay." I showed her then how the box worked.

"Hey, that's cool!" She took it from me and tried it herself, and her eyes lit up, and she smiled. But suddenly the smile disappeared. "But if it's Monse's box, he knows how to open it, and since he's the one who sneaks in and reads your notebook all the time, what good does it do?"

"I thought of that," I said. "I'll just have to find a hiding place for it. But at least now I don't have to worry if anybody else finds it—Mom or Daddy or anybody. Want to write something, some secrets or something? What did you do today?"

Mary Elizabeth looked at me for a long minute, then said, "Not much." She looked away and then

22

back, with a little smile. "Emily," she said slowly, "is that all you wanted me for, to show me a secret box?"

I felt my face get hot, and I quickly turned to the back window and looked out. I made up something fast, right on the spot. "No, that's not all. I wanted—well, you know, the coaches are—the kids are . . ." I was fumbling, and I stopped and collected my thoughts and rushed on. "The coaches are picking their team for the All-Stars this week. Mr. Wallin said so. I wanted to know if you wanted to practice."

There was a long silence, and I didn't turn around, but after a while Mary Elizabeth came over and stood by me at the window. "You know, Emily," she said, "I've been meaning to talk to you about the baseball—thing."

She paused, and I waited for her to go on, my heart beginning to pound hard.

"See," she continued. "I don't mean to hurt your feelings, but don't you think you're too old for baseball?"

"Too old!" I turned and stared at her, not even caring if my face was still red. "What do you mean, too old? You're the same age as me and you play baseball, too!"

"I know," she answered, "but that's what I'm trying to tell you. I'm not sure I want to play anymore this year."

"What!" I kept staring at her. We both play ball, we're the best kids on the team, and everybody knows it. There was hardly any doubt that we'd make the All-Stars, me as a pitcher and she as my catcher. How could she not play? "You're crazy," I said after a while.

"Not really. It is sort of childish."

"I don't believe you."

She just shrugged.

I turned to the window again and looked out. How could she, my best friend, not play? And if she didn't, how could I? Because she's the only one who knows my secret, that I'm scared of the ball, terrified of getting hit, so she's the only one I can have for a catcher. I looked at her once, quickly, and I guess tears started coming to my eyes because she poked my arm.

"Hey, don't get upset," she said. "I didn't say I wouldn't play. I just said I'm not sure."

I didn't answer, and she poked me again. "Come on, stop sulking."

"I'm not sulking," I answered. I wasn't either, but I was scared.

"Well, you're acting dumb. Come on, maybe I'll play till after the All-Stars."

I looked at her, not sure whether to believe her or not. And as if she had read my mind, she said, "I mean it, okay? If I get picked for the All-Stars, I'll play. After that . . ." She shrugged.

I let out my breath in a big puff. "Okay," I said slowly. I felt as if I had to hold onto this moment, keep her from changing her mind. "Okay, want to—do something?"

"Yeah, what?"

"Emily? Matthew?" It was Millie. "I'm home! Your mom and dad are home, too."

I turned from the window. Six o'clock, already?

Mary Elizabeth turned, too, and as she did, she looked at me and smiled, but it was a nice smile, not like that sarcastic one before. She giggled and put one hand to her mouth. "Emily, your mom and dad haven't seen you since you did that to your face?"

I shook my head. "Unh-unh."

She giggled again. "I hate to tell you this, but you look like a raccoon."

I went over and peered in the mirror. She was right—I was getting a really black eye. "Crumb," I said. "Mom's gonna have a fit, and I'm going to have to make up some story about how it happened."

"Yeah, well, don't blame me."

I made a face at her. "Want to stay awhile?" I asked. "It's not dinnertime yet. We could—do something." I thought of asking if she wanted to have a catch, but I didn't think I'd better do that just yet.

"Nope, I have to be home by six anyway. See you."

We both went into the hall then, and Mary Elizabeth started down the back stairs, but midway down she turned and grinned up at me. "Besides," she said softly, "I don't want to be around when your parents see that face."

"Thanks," I said, but I laughed.

"You're welcome," she said, and she laughed, too, and it was a nice sound. And then we smiled at each other, and we both said, "See ya," at the same time, just the way we always did.

3

I heard Mary Elizabeth say "Hello, Millie, good-bye, Millie. Hello, Mrs. Taylor, good-bye, Mrs. Taylor," and the screen door banged as she went out. I was about to start downstairs, but the phone began ringing, and I ran to Mom's room to answer it.

I picked up the phone. "Hello?"

"Hello, Emily?" It was Mr. Wallin, my baseball coach.

"Hi, Mr. Wallin!"

"Emily, think you could make a practice tonight at seven o'clock? I know it's last minute, but I have news for you, you and Mary Elizabeth."

"You do? What?" My heart began pounding hard. The All-Stars?

He laughed, as though he knew what I was thinking. "Yup, the All-Stars. I want you and Mary

Elizabeth both to play for me. I think you'd make a great pair."

"Wow!" I said. "Oh, wow, thanks!" I didn't add what I was thinking—what if Mary Elizabeth wouldn't play?

Mr. Wallin went on. "The game's not for three weeks yet, but since we take kids from different teams, the sooner we start to practice together, the better. You'll be there tonight?"

"Yeah, I'll be there."

"Good, see you then. I'm going to call Mary Elizabeth now."

"Good-bye," I said. "And thanks." To myself I added, "Good luck."

I hung up then and ran down the back stairs. "Mom! Daddy! Millie!" I shouted. "Guess what?"

They were all in the kitchen, reading the mail, and Daddy was taking off his jacket and tie—all the things they do when they first come home. Even Monse was there. He had just come in the back door with a big bag of groceries in his arms.

"Mom!" I said. "Guess what? Mr. Wallin called, and he said—"

"Emily!" Mom interrupted, staring at me.

"Emily!" Daddy said.

"Emily!" Millie said.

They all were looking at me, wide-eyed. I never realized their eyes were so blue. I could hear Mary Elizabeth's words floating around in my head: "I hate to tell you this, but you look like a raccoon."

"Emily, what happened to you?" Mom said.

I put one hand to my eye and touched it gently. "Nothing, it's just a bump." I looked over at Monse. "It's really nothing."

"Some 'nothing,' " Daddy said, and he started to laugh and then he said the same thing Mary Elizabeth had said, "You look like a raccoon."

Then Monse laughed, too, a big, loud horselaugh, and I glared at him.

But Mom and Millie weren't laughing, and Millie came over to me. "Now, how did you do that?" she scolded. "I leave you for an hour and you go get yourself hurt. I can't leave you, not even for a second—"

"It's all right, Millie." Mom interrupted her tirade. "It's only a black eye. But, Emily, how did you do it?"

Why hadn't I prepared a story? I began slowly, praying that something would come to me. "I—it was a door. See, we were playing—hide-'n'-seek! And I hid in my room, but when the door opened, it hit me. We were only fooling around."

" 'We' were fooling around?" Mom and Millie both said it at the same time. "Who's 'We'?"

I took one more quick look at Monse, and then I said the first name that jumped into my head. "Mary Elizabeth," I whispered.

I heard this little laugh from over where Monse was standing, and I looked at him quickly, but he was only standing there, examining the grocery bag very carefully.

"Now, if that isn't dumb," Millie said.

"It's no big deal," I answered. "It's just a black eye. But listen, guess what? I'm going to be on the All-Stars! Mr. Wallin just called, and I have a practice tonight at seven o'clock. And Mary Elizabeth is on the team, too."

"Congratulations, honey!" Mom said, and she smiled at me. "You've really wanted that, haven't you?"

I nodded and smiled, and Daddy came to me and ruffled up my hair and hugged me. He held me away then and grinned. "Well, I'm not really surprised. You are the greatest pitcher around."

"O-kay, Emily!" Monse said. "That's o-kay!"

I glared at him, but he seemed honest, like he really meant it, so I said, "Thanks."

"Well, it's nice," Millie said grudgingly, "but it would be nicer if you learned not to roughhouse when I'm not here." She turned then and went out to the yard and I made a face at her back.

Mom laughed softly. "Don't be upset, Emily. That's just Millie's way because she cares about you, that's all."

I shrugged.

"Come on." Mom looked at the clock. It was six-fifteen. "If you're going to get to your practice, we have to get you some dinner. But are you sure you're all right?"

"I'm sure, Mom. Just think, three weeks till All-Stars."

Mom went to the refrigerator then and began poking around inside. Over her shoulder she said, "I'll make you some hot dogs, and you set the table and make yourself a salad. The rest of us will eat later.''

Daddy went upstairs then, and Monse went outside, and Mom and I went to work on my dinner. "How was your day?" Mom asked while we were working.

"It was pretty good," I said. I wanted to tell her what Mary Elizabeth had said about maybe not playing ball anymore. Mom and I can talk about things like that, but I thought I'd wait till later when we had more time.

"Did you and Matt behave?" Mom said.

" 'Course," I answered. "Monse bugged me like he always does, but I ignored him, like you always tell me to."

"Emily," Mom said with a sigh, "I wish you would call your brother by his proper name. Matthew is a beautiful name, you know. Where did you ever get Monse from?"

"It's short for Monster," I answered, but I said it under my breath because I could never tell Mom why I call him that.

Mom sighed again, but she didn't say anything more. In a minute my hot dogs were ready, and Mom set them on the table. "I'm going upstairs to change now, but I'll be down in a minute. You start your dinner." She bent over me then and kissed my hair. "I'm happy for you," she said.

I smiled at her and took my hot dogs and sat down at the table by the window that looks over the backyard. It's so pretty out there. There are apple trees and a bird bath and flowers, and . . . Oh, no! Millie, and Mrs. Emory, Mary Elizabeth's mother, and Monse! They all were out by the fence, talking, and Millie was folding clothes from the line. Millie wouldn't tell Mrs. Emory what I said about Mary Elizabeth, would she? No, she wouldn't. But Monse would. Because even though I couldn't actually see it from here, I knew it—Monse was grinning.

I started to get up and go out there, but Millie and Monse were heading back to the house, and in a minute they were in the kitchen. Millie took the laundry to the laundry room, and the second she was gone, I said to Monse, "Did you tell? Did you say anything?"

He looked at me sheepishly. "Emily, honest, I didn't mean to. But you know Millie. She started talking and—"

I could hear Millie coming up the steps from the laundry room. "And you said Mary Elizabeth gave me a black eye?" I interrupted quickly.

"Not exactly," Monse answered. "I said you said it." He was grinning at me, and as Millie came into the kitchen, he winked and ran up the back stairs.

I was furious, but from the way he had grinned and then winked, I wasn't sure. Was he just teasing me again? I left the rest of my dinner and grabbed my cleats and glove and went out the back way. I shouted, "Good-bye," but I didn't go upstairs to see anybody. I ran down the drive to Mary Elizabeth's house, hoping that she'd had her dinner, hoping she was going to practice—hoping and praying that Monse hadn't told, that he'd only been teasing.

At the back screen door, I knocked, and almost instantly Mary Elizabeth opened it. "Yes?" she said as formally as if she'd never seen me before.

"Mary Elizabeth, did Mr. Wallin call you? He said we're both going to be on the All-Stars, that we'd make a great pair! Pitcher and catcher. And he said—" I stopped because she was still just looking at me. "I'm sorry," I said, and I was. "Monse told, didn't he? That I said it was you? I didn't mean to. It was just that he'd have taken the box back, and you were the first name that jumped into my head. But I never thought your mother would hear about—" I stopped; then very quietly I added, "Are you going to practice?"

Mary Elizabeth shook her head. "No way," she said. She looked angry, but her voice was trembling as if she were about to cry. "I'm not going to play baseball anymore. And if I did, I sure wouldn't play with someone who tells lies about their best friend!"

"But I didn't mean to . . ."

She didn't hear the rest of what I was going to say because she closed the door.

4

The next couple of days were the pits. The practice was lousy because when Mary Elizabeth didn't show up, Mr. Wallin put in Rob as my catcher. Rob acted as though he knew I was scared of the ball, and instead of just lobbing it back to me after a pitch, the way you're supposed to do to your pitcher, he threw it as hard as he could, and I missed it about a jillion times. Then, after the practice, Mr. Wallin had a talk with us about being scared of the ball, and although he didn't mention me by name, I knew who he was talking about.

But one thing was good—I was beginning to get an idea about how I could get even with Monse. My idea came at practice that night, when Mr. Wallin lectured us about being scared of the ball. "It's nothing to be ashamed of," he said. "Everybody's scared of something." And I knew what Monse was scared of—snakes—and I knew now I could get him. I would have to wait till Thursday, though, because that day Millie was having her hair done, so she wouldn't get there till late. That would give me the time I needed alone in the house. So, while I waited for Thursday, I wrote in my notebook a lot, but mostly I was lonely.

When Thursday morning came, as soon as Mom and Dad left for work, I went out in the back field and down by the stone wall with a paper bag under my arm. Lots of times I've seen snakes down there, dead ones and live ones, but now I wanted a dead one because it wouldn't move. I would get it, put it in the paper bag, and when Monse was out playing, I would sneak upstairs and put it in his bed. He would die of fright. They're just garter snakes, and they don't hurt anybody, but I remember once I showed one to Monse and he got so scared. . . .

"Yah!" Someone stuck his fingers in my ribs and shouted in my ear at the same time.

I spun around. It was Monse, grinning his stupid grin and wearing his stupid blue baseball hat and shirt. Even though my heart was pounding wildly, I tried to keep my face calm, and I held my nose and pointed to his shirt. "Don't you ever wash that?" I said.

He shrugged. "Sometimes."

"So, what are you doing out so early?"

"Following you. I've always wondered what vampires did when the sun came up."

"Ha, very funny."

"Not funny, it's true. You look like a vampire. Your face is getting all green."

"Yeah, thanks to you."

"Me? I didn't do anything, remember? It was Mary Elizabeth."

I couldn't answer, and I turned away, suddenly beginning to cry. Why was he always so mean? Why was he always teasing me? I kept my back turned because I couldn't let him see me cry.

"Hey, Emily?" he said behind me. "Want to have a catch? Practice for the All-Stars?"

"Unh, unh."

"Come on, I was just kidding you. Don't sulk."

"I'm not sulking!" Why does everybody always do that to me? First they tease me, and then they tell *me* not to sulk!

"Come on. I'll get the gloves and a ball. You need practice."

I still didn't turn around, but I was tempted. I wanted somebody to have a catch with. "Okay," I said finally.

Monse went up to the house then, and I watched him going, puzzled. How could he be like that? One minute he's teasing me, and the next he's nice. He was back in a minute with the ball and gloves, and he came over and handed me mine, but then he did something else—he gave me his baseball hat. He actually took it off and handed it to me! "Here, wear this for today," he said. "The brim will cover up enough so nobody will notice your black eye."

I took it from him, but I was too surprised even to answer. I turned it around in my hands, and it was yellow on the inside, with sweaty stains, but the outside looked okay. But it was his baseball hat! He hardly ever even takes it off.

"I mean it," he said. "Go ahead, try it."

Slowly I put it on, and Monse smiled. "You look like Joe Jock," he said.

I nodded thanks because I knew he meant it as a compliment.

He walked back across the field then and threw me the ball. I caught it easily and threw it back. We did it that way for a while, slow pitches, back and forth, but then Monse started throwing harder. I missed one ball and had to run after it, and then I missed the next one, too.

"Quit ducking!" Monse shouted once.

"I'm not ducking."

"You are, too."

"So would you if you were as scared as me," I muttered.

Monse threw the ball again, and this time I did duck because I could see it coming, right at my head. I closed my eyes.

Monse stopped throwing. "If you don't get your body in front of the ball, you're never going to be a good player."

"Yeah, and if I do get my body in front of the ball, I'm going to be a dead player. Suppose I miss it and it hits me?"

"Doesn't hurt."

"Huh?" I shouted it. "You're nuts."

Monse took off his glove and came over to me. "Well, maybe it does a little, but you know what's worse?"

"What?"

"Letting it control your life. Letting it turn you into a chicken."

"Who says it's worse? And anyway, what's that mean?"

"It means if you want to play ball but can't play right because you're scared, you're letting the fear control your life. Listen, if you promise not to tell anybody, I'll tell you something."

"What? I won't tell."

"Well, remember a few summers ago when I couldn't hit the ball for beans? Daddy and my coach kept trying to teach me how to bat—how to hold the bat and proper batting stance and all that. But it wasn't that I didn't know how; it was that I was scared of the ball, just like you."

He paused and looked at me, and I didn't argue with him, saying that "just like you" part, but I didn't answer him either. But he kept looking at me for so long, as though he were waiting for something, that I finally said, "Go ahead."

"So," he continued, "I got hit once, and everybody came running out on the field and asking if I was all right, and I couldn't answer them, not because I was hurt that much, but because I realized I *wasn't* hurt that much. See, it wasn't nearly as bad as I thought it would be. And after that I was never much scared anymore. It didn't control me any-more."

I looked at him, feeling the way I do sometimes when Mom is giving me one of her talks about how things work out for the best or something. I could hardly believe he was my brother, my thirteen-year-old brother! But I wasn't so sure he knew what he was talking about either.

"So," he continued quietly, "if you want to play, you just have to hang in there, scared and all."

I wasn't sure that I could hang in there, or even that I wanted to, but I knew he was trying to help me. "Yeah, Matt," I said. "I guess. But I'm still scared."

"I know." He walked back across the field and started to throw the ball again, but he didn't throw it quite so hard. "It's okay to be scared"—he grinned at me—"as long as you keep your body in front of the ball."

5

We threw for a while longer, but pretty soon Monse tucked his glove under his arm. "I'm starved. I'm getting breakfast," he said. "Want to come?"

I shook my head, suddenly remembering what I had come out here for. But I felt kind of guilty now, thinking about that. I took off Matt's baseball cap and held it out to him. "Want your hat back?"

He shook his head. "Nope, you can wear it today. You need it." He turned and started up to the house.

"Hey, Matt?" I called after him.

He turned around. "What?"

"Thanks," I said.

"It's okay." He smiled at me.

I went farther down the field then, but I didn't look for snakes right away. Instead, I sat on the stone wall, thinking, kicking my sneakers back and forth against the wall, watching tiny pebbles dislodge. Monse had been really nice. . . . And right there, right beneath me, I saw it—a long yellow spotted snake. It was dead, at least it wasn't moving, and I kicked it a little just to be sure, and it still didn't move. I couldn't resist.

I reached in the pocket of my jeans, pulled out some crumpled-up tissues. They had been there so long they were really thin, and little bits of dust came floating up from them but they were better than nothing. I bent over the snake, and very carefully, with my fingers protected by the tissues, I picked it up. It was gross. Even with my fingers covered like that, I could feel it underneath, round and slippery. I swallowed hard to keep from throwing up, but I moved fast and dropped the snake, tissues and all, in the bag. And then I laughed out loud. Even if Monse had been nice to me before, I could just picture him, climbing into bed on top of a snake!

I took the bag then and ran up to the house, and right away I noticed two things—Millie's car wasn't there yet, and there were three bikes out back, Monse's and two of his friends. The bikes each had a baseball glove and cleats hung around the handlebars, so that would mean that Monse was probably on his way to practice. And with Millie not here yet, I'd have just the chance I wanted.

I didn't go into the house then but instead went to the garage to hide the bag in a corner there until Monse was gone. Then, while I waited, I got out the lawn mower and went out to the front. Daddy said last night that Monse and I had to do our lawns today before we did anything else. I have to mow the front once every week, and Monse has to do the back one. The back is bigger than the front, and Monse complains, but I don't mind much because we have one of those ride-on mowers, and I kind of like using it.

Out in front, I began checking the lawn for rocks and sticks. It's one of Daddy's rules about the mower—that we have to clear any stones or anything because if the mower blade hit a rock, it could make it fly up and hurt us. Daddy's other rule about the mower is that we can't use it unless a grown-up is at home, so while I waited for Millie, I decided to get the lawn cleared and get it over with. I still had Monse's baseball cap on, and it felt good, keeping the sun off my face. I was just about finished picking up when I heard the mower going, and I looked up. It was Monse, sitting on the mower, heading for the back lawn!

"Hey!" I shouted. "I'm using that!" I ran after him. I knew he couldn't hear me—you can't hear anything when you're on that mower—so I ran fast and caught up with him, then shook his sleeve. "I'm using that!" I shouted in his ear as loud as I could.

"What?" he shouted back.

I could tell from the way he was grinning that he knew what I was saying. "I . . . was . . . using . . . that!" I screamed it.

"Oh." He turned the mower off. "Well, how did I know?"

"Because it was right out there in front and it wasn't in the garage and I was checking for stones, and you know it!"

"Ah, come on, let me use it first, please? Dad said I had to do the lawn before I went to my game, and I have *practice* first." He said "practice" the way some people say "God," but I shook my head.

"No, I had it first."

In a softer voice then, he said, "I lent you my hat. I'll even let you wear it when I go to practice. And I'll have another catch with you later, okay?"

He could see that I was softening, and he added, "Come on, Rich and Joe left for practice already!"

I waited another minute, but then I said, "Okay, okay."

"Thanks." He smiled at me.

"Hey, wait a minute!" I suddenly remembered something. "You're not allowed. Millie's not here yet."

"Doesn't matter. It won't take long, and I'll get it done before she ever gets here."

"But Daddy says we're not allowed to. What if he finds out?"

Monse shrugged. "How's he going to find out?" He looked at me then, and I guess we both had the same idea at the same time because he said warningly, slowly, "Em-il-y. I did you a favor, Emily."

"All right, all right," I said. I grinned, though, and

43

Monse looked at me, as if this time he was the one who wasn't sure whether or not I was teasing. But then he turned the mower back on and started down the back lawn.

I went into the garage and got the paper bag, then went up to the house. Quietly I tiptoed up the back stairs to the third floor and into Monse's room. Boy, I felt creepy in there, thinking what would happen if I got caught. But I could still hear the mower running from outside, and as long as I could hear that, I'd know I was safe. I went over to Monse's bed and turned back the blankets and bedspread, then turned over the paper bag and shook it. The snake slid out and plopped into bed.

I shivered, but I laughed out loud. A snake in bed! Then I pulled the covers back up, leaving them all lumpy the way they were before so he wouldn't notice anything different. I was still laughing when I ran downstairs to the kitchen for my breakfast.

In the kitchen I could still hear the lawn mower running, but it sounded kind of funny, a low, quiet hum, not rumbling the way it usually does. I hoped it wasn't running out of gas just when it was my turn to mow. I dug in the refrigerator, looking for something good, then decided to skip breakfast and have lunch because there were all the things I like for my favorite sandwich. I got bologna, some leftover chicken, pickles, lettuce, tomato, and I made toast and put everything on it—with mustard, mayonnaise and Russian dressing on top. Perfect! I took it all to the table, then sat down by the window, looking out.

That was weird! The mower was way down by the field, its front pressing against the stone wall. It was running—I could hear it—but Monse wasn't on it.

I took a bite of my sandwich, then went out on the back steps. "Monse?" I called. "Monse?" Daddy would be really mad if he knew the mower was running and nobody was watching it.

He didn't answer, and I looked around the yard. Was he down there somewhere picking up stones? I hadn't seen him clear the lawn before he started.

"Monse?" I called again. "Monse?"

Boy, would Daddy be mad! And if Millie got here and saw it, Monse would be in more trouble than anything.

I still didn't see him anywhere, but I knew I'd better turn off the mower, so I started down the yard. I was halfway down when the wasps came after me. There were two of them, and they kept buzzing around my head. "Cut it out!" I screamed at them, as if they could understand. They did, or at least, when I waved my hand, they flew away. One of them followed me a little way, but then it was gone, too. I was looking over my shoulder to be sure it wasn't still following me—so I almost stepped on him.

When I first saw him lying there, I thought he was teasing me. He was doing this to tease! He was lying in the grass, and there was blood—all over him. His eyes were closed, and his face was blue, sort of white with blue spots all over it. There was blood everywhere. He wasn't moving.

"Monse!" I screamed. "Monse!"

I bent over him. He was doing it on purpose! He knew I was scared of blood. "Matt!" I screamed again. "Stop it!"

He didn't move, didn't blink or open his eyes. He didn't even grin at me. His blue baseball shirt was covered with blood.

"Monse, Monse, stop it! Please, stop it."

He still didn't move. He wasn't fooling.

"Please, Monse, please? Please, open your eyes."

6

I didn't know what to do. Millie wasn't here yet. Mom and Daddy weren't here—nobody! "Monse!" I bent over him, grabbed his shoulders, and tried to pull him up, but he fell back to the ground. "Monse, open your eyes, please? Please stop!"

I put both arms around him, lifted him, and held him there for a minute, trying to get him to talk to me. "Monse, what's the matter?" But he didn't respond, only lay heavily against me. I tried to drag him, get him back to the house, but he was too heavy, and I had to lay him back down. "Monse, please stop it!"

I left him there and ran to the house. Who should I call? Mom and Daddy, they were at work. Millie? The doctor? I saw the number on the phone, the emergency number, 911. I dialed it. "My brother's hurt," I said. I think I was crying. I gave them the address, then ran out to the yard.

Monse was still lying there, his eyes still closed. There was something that had to be done—what? The tractor—that's what I had to do, turn off the tractor before anybody got here and knew. I started down to the wall, but as I ran, the tractor stopped all by itself.

I ran back to Monse, bent over him, called his name. "Monse, *please*?"

The policeman came first, and I motioned to him. He stopped the car and came running across the grass. Millie's car came after him, and then, right after, the ambulance. It was a big white one, its siren screaming, the lights flashing. The policeman waved to the driver of the ambulance, and the ambulance came across the lawn to us. It didn't even use the driveway, came right across the grass! Daddy would be so mad, would—

The driver and another man jumped out. One of them had a black bag in his hand, and they both bent over Monse. Then they stood up and looked at me. They bent back down.

Nobody spoke. It was quiet, like at church. I looked at Millie, standing there, pale, wide-eyed, holding her hand over her throat. I thought she would start to yell the way she always does when one of us gets hurt, but she just stood, staring down at Monse, her mouth open as if to scream, but no sound came out.

Across the drive I saw a neighbor, Mrs. Churchill, come out, then Mrs. Emory and then Mary Elizabeth. Mrs. Emory came over, spoke to Millie, something about Mom and Daddy. Then she ran back to the house, and I felt better because I knew she was calling them.

The ambulance men were doing things to Monse, pressing big white bandages against his arms, wrapping them. One of them lifted up his shirt, and there was blood everywhere, even on his stomach. They put a needle in his arm.

The policeman spoke to Millie then, quietly, and it was weird, as though it were happening in slow motion, as though it were somewhere else, maybe on TV. As though it were not happening here. Then they finished wrapping the bandages, but Monse still hadn't opened his eyes, although I knew he would in a minute. They slid him onto a stretcher, then covered him up with a big gray blanket. And then I knew I had to stop them.

"No!" I grabbed the ambulance man's arm. "Stop it! You can't do that to him. It's so hot out here in the sun. He'll be too hot."

The man just shook his head at me, but still, he didn't speak. He lifted my hand gently from his arm and turned back to Monse. Together they wrapped some straps around him, tying him to the stretcher, but even then he didn't move, didn't open his eyes or grin at me. The men lifted up the stretcher, slid it into the ambulance, and then one of them climbed in back with Monse. The other closed the two big doors, then turned the handle on the outside, as though they were locking him in.

The driver got in then, and the ambulance started slowly back across the grass, then down the drive. The siren wasn't screaming anymore, but the yellow light was on, going silently around and around.

I looked at Millie, at the neighbors, who were lined up across the drive. Even from here I could see Mary Elizabeth's face. It was pure, dead white. But it was the policeman who looked the oddest, sort of like the ambulance man for that second that he looked at me, almost as if he were going to cry. He put his arm around my shoulder and nodded with his head in the direction of the house. "Come with me?" he said. He motioned to Millie, too, as though he were inviting her. "Come up to the house. We'll wait for your parents up there."

I walked back across the lawn with Millie and the policeman, and Mrs. Emory came up behind. She spoke quietly to me. "Would you like to go down and stay with Mary Elizabeth for a while? Until your mom gets home?"

I shook my head. Not now.

When we got to the house, the policeman asked if I could tell him what happened. How could I when I didn't know? So I told him how I had looked out the window because the mower sounded funny and how I saw it down by the fence, but that Monse wasn't on it. And I didn't know how he could have fallen off or how he got cut like that. "Why was he bleeding like that?" I asked.

The officer shook his head. "I don't know." But he looked at Millie then, and it was one of those *looks*, like Mom and Daddy have sometimes, and I knew right away that they weren't telling me something.

Softly Millie began to cry.

"What?" I said, and I was crying too. "What happened to him, do you know?"

The policeman put his hand on my shoulder, but I shook it off. "What happened? Do you *know*?"

I must have said it very loudly because Millie came and put her arms around me. "Hush," she said. "Hush, it's all right."

"It's not all right! You know something."

"I think—" Millie stopped, put a hand to her throat. "It must have been the mower."

"The mower? You mean the mower *ran over him*?"

Neither Millie nor the policeman answered me or looked at me, but Millie nodded. And I began to laugh. They were being silly! The mower couldn't have run over Monse; it couldn't. That's really dangerous. Daddy's always telling us that, and that's why he won't let us use the mower unless a grown-up is home. Like, I remember the time Monse and I were fooling around with the mower, pretending we were in a parade, only we were fighting over who would steer it, and Daddy caught us and he was so angry, because he said we could get *killed* that way—

Oh, no! That's not what they were thinking, was

it? I looked at them. They weren't thinking that Monse was . . . That was dumb. Not Monse. Not dead.

"I have to go to the bathroom," I said. Upstairs. Away. Quick. Not dead. Not *dead*.

I ran upstairs, into my room, closed the door, and fell facedown on my bed. Monse was hurt, I knew he was hurt, but it was just a cut! Maybe even a bad cut, but just a cut. Anyway, the ambulance men were taking care of him, good care, and they'd take care of him at the hospital. That's where he was now with Mom and Daddy, and he was probably right now showing off, bragging about his ambulance ride.

I sat up. That's all it was, a bad cut, maybe even needing stitches, maybe even a lot of stitches, something for Monse to show off about. He wasn't dead. Millie just always gets superupset about things like that, making a big fuss, just the way she did over my black eye. I looked at my watch. It was eleven o'clock, time for Matt's practice. I hoped it wasn't his pitching arm he cut.

And then I remembered . . . the snake. I flew up the stairs to Monse's room, grabbed it from his bed, opened his window, and dropped it into the grass. Then I ran back to my room. Kneeling down alongside my bed, I got out the box and secret notebook and a pen and began to write. "Monse got hurt today," I wrote. "I don't know how bad it is, but it's probably not bad. Just some stitches, but boy, will he show off! He'll be home soon with Mom and Dad."

I closed the book then, put it in the box, then stuck the box way back under the bed so Monse wouldn't find it. Then I went in the bathroom and looked in the mirror and was surprised to see I was still wearing Monse's baseball cap. That was good because I'd save it for him, for when he came home.

7

When I got downstairs, the policeman wasn't in the kitchen anymore, but through the window I could see him sitting in his police car, writing something. Mrs. Emory and Mrs. Churchill were there, though, one on either side of Millie, talking to her quietly. They stopped when I came in, and Mrs. Emory looked up and spoke to me. "Emily, come down with me to my house. All of us can go and wait for your mom and daddy there."

I shook my head. I didn't want to go to her house. Didn't want to see Mary Elizabeth. I wanted to wait right here until Mom and Daddy came back with Monse. "No, thank you, Mrs. Emory," I said. "I have to wait here. With Millie."

But Millie only shook her head. She hadn't said one word since she got here—except what she said before about the mower—and she still didn't speak. She just shook her head slowly, back and forth, and tears were running down her cheeks. Her eyes were so swollen they were almost shut, and Mrs. Emory wrapped her arms around Millie and pulled her close. "Come," she said really softly, as if she were talking to a very small child, and although she looked at me, I didn't know if she was talking to Millie or to me.

I didn't want to go to her house, but I couldn't stand being with Millie like that either, so I just nodded. Then the four of us went out the back door.

As we went across the back field, a wasp buzzed at me again, and I ducked away from it. I could see another wasp circling Mrs. Churchill's head, and she ducked, too, and it flew away.

When we got to the Emorys' house, Mary Elizabeth was in the kitchen. She looked at me quickly and then looked away, and I couldn't tell from that look whether she was still mad at me or not. I wasn't sure if I was mad or not either, but I did know that I didn't want to talk about baseball and fights right now.

Mrs. Emory and Mrs. Churchill led Millie to a chair and sat her down, and then Mrs. Emory began making tea. She got out pots and cups and tea and milk, but she seemed confused, and every little while she stopped and put one hand on her chest, as though holding her heart. Once she saw me standing there, and she looked surprised, as though she had forgotten me. "Emily! Dear!" she said. She came to me. "What can I do for you? Would you like some—ice cream?"

"No, thank you."

She put down the teapot then and stood in front of me, her hands hanging awkwardly at her sides. For a minute I was afraid she was going to hug me, but then she only reached out and put one hand against my cheek for a second. "TV?" she said. "Watch TV?" She sounded helpless.

I nodded, and from across the room Mary Elizabeth said, "Yeah." And we both raced out of the kitchen, relieved to be out of there for now. But we didn't speak to each other, and in the family room Mary Elizabeth turned on the TV.

Some stupid game show was on, but it didn't matter what it was because we weren't really watching it anyway. We just sat, staring dumbly, but then someone on the show did something stupid—jumped up in the air and kissed somebody at the same time—and I laughed out loud.

Mary Elizabeth giggled, too, and it was such a nice, friendly, familiar sound that I couldn't help looking at her. She looked at me, too, and then looked away. "Mr. Wallin called yesterday," she said softly.

"Yeah?"

"Yeah, he asked again if I would play on the All-Stars."

"Yeah?" I said again.

She was quiet for a long time. "I don't know if I want to play—with you."

I shrugged.

There was another long silence while we turned back to the TV, but then Mary Elizabeth spoke again. "Well, why did you do that, tell my mother that I gave you a black eye? Just so you could keep some stupid secret box? That was mean. I'd never do that to you."

For a minute I didn't know what she was talking about. Didn't she know that I didn't tell her mother? I would never do that. "I didn't tell her that," I said finally. "It was Monse."

"What?" Mary Elizabeth whirled around. "You mean that Monse told my mother that I gave you a black eye just to cover for himself?"

"No," I said. "He didn't do it to cover for himself. He did it—I'm not sure why, but maybe he was just teasing. See, I told my parents that it was you, so it was really my fault, but I knew they'd never tell your mom. But then I saw Monse outside talking to her, and I guess he was just teasing us both."

Mary Elizabeth looked disgusted. "He's a jerk, a real jerk. How can you stand him?"

I jumped up—and I slapped her hard, right in the face. "He's not a jerk, he's not a jerk!" I shouted. "He's—my brother!"

There was a long silence while the two of us stared at each other, Mary Elizabeth with one hand to her face, holding it where I had hit her. I could see her face getting red around it and her eyes filling up with tears, and I was sorry. I hadn't meant to do that, but I couldn't say so. She had no right to say that about Monse. He didn't do it to be mean. He was only fooling. . . .

Both of us heard it at the same time—the voices in the kitchen. Not Mrs. Churchill and Mrs. Emory and Millie, but other voices, quiet ones—Mom and Daddy!

I ran to the kitchen.

Mom was beside Millie, holding her hands, and Daddy was holding both their hands. Mom's face was white, really white, and her eyes all red from crying, and Daddy had been crying, too.

"Mom?" I said.

Mom let go of Millie's hands and came to me, both arms out, and Daddy came, too. Mom put her arms around me, and Daddy put his arms around the both of us. Monse? How is Monse?

I couldn't ask, couldn't say it. No matter how hard I tried, the words just didn't come out.

We stood like that for a long time, and suddenly there was a sound, a tearing, ripping sound—a sob. Daddy was sobbing! I pulled away and looked at him.

He was crying, tears rolling down his cheeks and running around the corners of his mouth.

Mom? Her eyes were filled with tears, and her mouth was in a funny, tight line, as though she were holding something in.

I wanted to say it—how is Matt? But still, I couldn't. I put my arms around Mom again, pulled close, and buried my head in her chest. I didn't want to see their faces. I wiggled, trying to get deeper in their arms, pulling on Daddy to wrap his arms around the two of us again. But he didn't, and Mom didn't, and after a minute Mom pushed me away gently.

She scrunched down in front of me, the way she used to when I was just a little kid, and tears were running down her face. "Emily?" she said. "Matt is dead."

"I know," I said. I pulled away from her. I didn't know. Monse wasn't dead, but I had to say that, because it was the only way to make her stop telling me, I knew that. I started to walk out of the Emorys' kitchen. I thought for a minute they would stop me, but nobody said anything.

I went down the back steps, across the field, up to our house. A wasp chased me again—two wasps. I ducked away from them. I didn't run. I just waved them away. I got to the house. I went in. The wasps stayed outside.

Very slowly I went up the back stairs to my room, closed my door, then went over to the bed. I took out the black box from underneath, got out the notebook, found a pen, sat down on the bed. I had to be very careful. If I wrote it just right, then everything would be all right. I picked up the pen and began slowly. "Mom and Daddy are back from the hospital," I wrote. "Monse has to . . . Monse will stay there awhile. He needs . . . stitches. Daddy says. Daddy says he has to rest for a while. He's going to miss his game today. I hope he makes it home. In time for the next one."

■■■■■ 8 ■■■■■

For a long time after, I stayed in my room. Sounds
came up from downstairs, people coming and going
and the phone ringing practically all the time, but I
stayed there with the door locked. Once I took out
the secret box and put Monse's baseball hat in it,
and I looked at the notebook, but I didn't write anything because I couldn't think of anything to say that
would make any difference. So I pushed the box
back under the bed, and then I went to the window,
trying to push back other things, like thoughts,
things like that. But outside the window I could see
Mom and Daddy and the policeman walking around
in the field, and I turned away from that, too. Matt,
where was Matt? I couldn't believe it was true.
People don't die, not just like that, not your *brother*.

   After a while there was a knock on my door, and I

knew right away who it was. "Go away," I said. I said it firmly, but I tried not to sound mean.

"Emily?" Daddy called. "Can I come in?"

"No, I'm busy."

"Please, Emily?" It was Mom, and the doorknob rattled. "Please let us come in. We want to see you, honey."

What should I do? If I let them in, they'd start talking about it again. But I had to, and I knew it, so slowly I got off the bed and went and unlocked the door.

They both came in then, looking really awful, Mom especially. Usually she's so pretty, but now she was pale, and her eyes so swollen you could barely see them. Daddy came to me and pulled me close, and Mom reached for me, too.

They hugged me silently for a while, but after a minute I pulled away. And even though I had promised myself never to ask it, never to talk about it, it was the first thing I said. "Daddy, what happened to Monse? How did he get cut?"

Daddy swallowed hard and pushed a hand through his hair. "It was the mower." He bent close to me then, scrunched down in front of me just as Mom had done before, as though I were a little kid. "Emily, can you tell us what happened? Did you see him fall, anything?" He was looking hard into my face, intently, as though he were willing me to say something, but I didn't know what it was.

"No!" I shook my head. "I didn't see anything,

didn't hear anything. I just noticed the mower sounded funny at first."

Daddy looked away from me and up at Mom, and I looked, too. They both nodded, as though they were agreeing about something. "And did you go to check?" Daddy asked very quietly.

"Not at first!" I stopped. "I mean—" Oh, if I had checked right away—is that what they were thinking?

"What, honey?" Daddy said.

"I just heard it sounding funny." I took a deep breath and raced on because I couldn't think, not for a second, that it was my fault. "I looked outside, and the mower was down by the fence, but Monse wasn't on it. Daddy! Millie said the mower ran over him. It didn't, did it?"

"It did," Daddy said.

"But how?" I cried. "How could he do that? Monse wouldn't fall off a lawn mower!"

Again Daddy looked at Mom, and again they both nodded, and this time Daddy pulled me so close I couldn't see his face, and he spoke into my hair. "We know how, honey. See, Mom and the policeman and I went down into the field. There was a wasps' nest—sand wasps." He paused, and I could feel his arms around me tighten.

"So?" I said. "I saw wasps, so what?"

"At the hospital they found that Matt had a lot of wasp or bee stings on his—body. We think he ran into a wasps' nest." He stopped again, then continued speaking in little spurts. "And the wasps attacked him. And if he was trying to get away, he jumped, or he fell. And the mower ran over him." He paused once more, his arms getting so tight around me my ribs were beginning to hurt. . . . "And he bled to death." He said that last sentence softly, almost as though he were talking to himself.

"But that's stupid, it's dumb! He didn't scream, anything. Monse isn't stupid; he wouldn't just lie there and bleed. . . . He's not stupid!" I pulled away from Daddy angrily.

"That's what we wanted to ask you, Emily," Mom said, and she sounded hesitant, the way Daddy had when he started. "You didn't hear him, he didn't call, anything?"

"No, he didn't call or anything! He didn't—" I stopped.

"What?" They both were looking at me.

"Nothing," I said. "It was nothing." But I was thinking—I was up in Monse's room, up on the third floor, putting a snake in his bed. I wouldn't have heard him. You can't hear anything from up there. A tight place began to form in my chest, getting tighter and tighter.

Daddy walked away from me then and looked out the window. "One more thing, Emily, if you can. Do you know why Matt was using the mower when Millie wasn't here? He knows the rules."

Right away I knew what I had to say. "He didn't know she wasn't here, I guess."

"But he was supposed to find out. It wasn't like him not to."

"I guess he was in a hurry, and he didn't notice. See, he had to do the lawn before he went to his practice. You told him that last night." I didn't care if I was lying; I couldn't let them be mad at Matt.

Daddy leaned his head against the windowpane. "Oh," he moaned softly. "I never should have let you children use the mower. Never."

Mom went to him and rested her forehead against his back. "It's not your fault," she said firmly. "Now stop that. If anything, it's my fault. I told you I had the feeling I should have stayed until Millie came today."

Daddy turned to Mom, and they held each other, and I stared at them. They both came to me, and we had a big hug, wrapping our arms around one another. But I felt stiff, as though I were made of ice, and I knew I had to push everything away, everything I was thinking. I looked through their arms and out through the window. It was sunny outside. There was baseball, the All-Stars. In just three weeks I'd play in the All-Stars, and I didn't even care if Mary Elizabeth played or not; I could play just fine without her. Mr. Wallin said I was a great player, and even Monse had said, "You're okay. That's okay, Emily!"

Mom was saying something to me. "Honey?" She held me away and looked at me. "Did you hear me?"

I shook my head because I hadn't heard her, hadn't heard anything but my own thoughts. "I'm going to play baseball. I'm going to play in the All-Stars."

"Would you come downstairs now, Emily?" Mom said. "We need to talk, all of us, as a family. We need to make plans for Matt's—funeral."

"No." I shook my head and spoke quietly. "No, Mommy." I hadn't called her that since I was little, and I didn't know why I said it now. "I can't come downstairs. You—do it." Because suddenly in my head, I had a plan, a plan so simple I knew I could make it work.

Mom looked at Daddy, and they both nodded, as if they understood. Daddy stroked my hair. "It's okay, sweetheart," he said. "But come down later, when you feel that you can, all right?"

I nodded, but I knew I wouldn't go downstairs, not ever, not now, not until Matt came home. When they went out of my room, I closed the door quietly behind them, went to my bed, got out the secret box and the notebook, sat down on the bed, and began to write. "Monse got run over by the lawn mower today," I wrote. "And stung by wasps, too. Poor Monse, he must feel awful. But in a few days Daddy says he'll feel better, and then they'll bring him home. Maybe I'll even go to one of his games when he gets here. And in three weeks I play in the All-Stars. Maybe he'll come watch me, and maybe that day I'll pitch a no-hitter for him."

When I finished, I put away the notebook, got my

pajamas out of the dresser, put them on, and climbed into bed. It was still light out, but it didn't matter. I would go to sleep, and it would all go away, just the way everything used to get better when I was little. I would go to sleep, and in the morning everything would be just the same, just the way it was this morning. Monse would be home, and he'd be teasing me, and we'd have a catch again. Just as he promised.

9

When I woke next, the sun was bright, and the house noisy, as though everyone were up and moving around. A shower was running, and somewhere I could hear Mom and Daddy talking softly. I looked at my clock—nine o'clock! What were they doing home at this hour? Was it Saturday? I jumped out of bed. It must be Saturday! Then Daddy was going to take me and Monse—

The pain hit in the center of my chest, hard, when I began to remember. I folded my arms quickly across it, to keep something inside there from breaking. I started to go to the bathroom, but my heart was racing, and I felt faint and sick, too, and I didn't know which way to go. Carefully I eased myself back onto the bed and tugged at the blanket till it covered me again. When I was lying down, the faintness began to go away, but what was I going to do? It was morning—was Matt still dead?

There was a knock on my door, and I didn't answer, and there was another. The door opened, and Mom called softly. "Emily, are you awake?" She came in and sat on the bed. "Do you want to get up now?"

I shook my head, just a little, because I was afraid the faint feeling would come back, but I didn't open my eyes to look at her.

"Emily?" Mom waited for me to answer.

"What?"

"I know you feel awful, terrible, we all do. But you can't run away from it, honey."

"I'm not running away, I'm sick. Please leave me alone."

"Emily, sit up for a minute."

I knew she'd wait until I did, so I took the blanket off and slowly sat up. Mom looked awful, pale and lined. In some funny corner of my mind, I thought suddenly that she looked like Nana used to look, as if overnight she had stopped being my mother and become my grandmother. And I knew that tomorrow or some other time I'd have to think about how it could happen like that.

Mom began stroking my hair gently. "Emily," she said. "We've made some arrangements. We're going to have a wake today. You remember what that is, like when Nana died? We're going to have it at the same funeral home, and tomorrow we'll have the funeral. We've called the family, and Aunt Ann and Uncle Ed are on their way and—'' She stopped, I guess because I was shaking my head furiously. It made the room spin, but I didn't care. They couldn't do that to Monse, not a funeral!

"What, Emily?"

"No, you can't do that! I mean, I'm not—not going!" I lay back down and yanked the covers over me again.

"Oh, honey!" Mom half lay down next to me and put her arms around me.

"You can't, it's not fair!" I whispered into her shoulder.

"Tell me," Mom said. "Tell me what you mean."

"No." I shook my head because even though I knew, I couldn't tell her; she wouldn't understand. It was because if I went, if I saw him there—like I saw Nana that time—then he might really be dead. And I couldn't do that to him.

"Honey, please talk to me?" Mom sounded so sad, and I wanted to help her, but I couldn't. I held the covers tightly, afraid she'd try to take them off and make me get up, but she didn't. It was silent for so long that for a minute I thought Mom had gone out of the room, but then I could tell that she was still sitting beside me. She began rubbing my back very softly, and I think I fell asleep that way.

When I woke next, it was twelve o'clock. I had turned over in my sleep, and now I was facing right into the clock on my bedside table. I lay there, staring, trying to remember. Why did I feel sad? Was it baseball, the All-Stars; did I make the All-Stars?

Yes, I did, so baseball was all right. Mary Elizabeth, is that what it was? Yeah, she was still mad at me. . . .

I looked up. Someone was sitting next to my bed, looking at me, smiling just a little. Daddy! He had pulled my desk chair over and was right next to me. He was all dressed up, as if he were going to work, with his new suit and shirt and dark tie, and he looked really good—except for his face. He looked awful, like Mom had looked, like an old nana, and then I remembered, and the pain was there. But Daddy just smiled at me, and he brushed some hair from my forehead. "Hi, sleepyhead," he said. "Do you feel better? You were sure sleeping soundly."

I nodded and looked away, or tried to look away, but it was hard to do without turning over and turning my back on him, and I didn't want to hurt his feelings.

"I've been sitting here, watching you for the last hour," Daddy said. "You sure can sleep."

An hour? Why had he been watching me for an hour?

"How do you feel?" Daddy said.

"Sick."

"Really sick?"

I nodded.

"Are you well enough to get up? We really need you. It's time to go to the funeral home." When I didn't answer, he said, "Are you listening, honey?"

I nodded, but the thing that was in my chest crept up into my throat.

"Mommy told you. The wake is today, and the funeral tomorrow. We've been able to get them to open a grave—"

"No, *no!*" Suddenly not only could I talk, but I screamed at him. Why was he doing this to me? Why was he in my room, talking to me, watching me even when I was asleep? Couldn't I have any privacy? Why didn't he leave me alone? I wasn't going to any funeral, any grave! Monse wasn't even dead! "I'm sick!" I shouted at him. "Why don't you leave me alone? Can't you see I'm sick?"

Suddenly Mom appeared in the doorway, and she looked quickly from me to Daddy, and then she came to us.

I watched her come in, then looked at Daddy, then sat up suddenly, holding my hand tight over my mouth. I was going to throw up, I could feel it coming, and I jumped out of bed and ran for the bathroom. Mom ran with me, and I leaned over the toilet and threw up for a long time. Mom held a wet washcloth to my face and kept wiping my face and neck with it, and it felt really good.

Then, as fast as the throwing up had come, something else happened. The room and everything around me started to get dark, moving in from around the edges of the room until it was all black. I could feel the floor moving away, and I think I fainted.

I was lying in my bed. Mom and Daddy were there, and somebody else, sitting on the edge of my bed—Dr. Walker, the one who's been taking care of me ever since I was a baby. "Emily," she said quietly when she saw me awake.

I didn't answer, and she laid a hand against my forehead, pushing my hair back gently, the way Daddy does sometimes. "Can you tell me what happened? Do you hurt anywhere?"

I nodded. "Everywhere."

"Show me."

I put a hand to my chest, and Dr. Walker turned the covers back and began pressing my chest and stomach. I tried to twist away from her, but she kept one hand firmly against my chest. "Emily, it's important. Please, hold still and let me look at you."

I knew there was no sense arguing with her, and I lay with my eyes closed, letting her poke at me, lying very still as if I were dead. What was it like to be dead? Could you feel anything? Was everything black? Could he see, could he move? Where was he?

Dr. Walker made me sit up, and she checked my back and then my legs and even the soles of my feet. She spent a long time looking inside my eyes. After a while she let me lie back down. "I don't find too much wrong," she said. She looked at Mom and Dad and then back at me. "Do you think you could get up now?"

"No." What did she mean, there wasn't much wrong? Couldn't she see how sick I was?

"Matt's funeral is tomorrow," she said, as normally as if she were saying, "There's a baseball game tomorrow." "Do you think you'll be well enough to get up by then?"

I shook my head, afraid that if I spoke, I'd scream at her, just like I did at Daddy before.

"Why, Emily?"

Why? Was she crazy? What kind of doctor was she? She wanted to know why I couldn't go to Matt's funeral—when he wasn't even dead? I shook my head, closed my eyes, and prayed silently: Go away, just go away, please?

"You could go right back to bed afterwards," she persisted. And when I still didn't answer her, she said, "All right then. It's all right." She patted me and tucked the cover around me a little, and then she got up off the bed and went to where Mom and Daddy were standing.

The three of them stood together in a corner of my room for a long time, talking about me quietly, but I could hear every word they were saying. It was as if I wasn't even there, the way they talked. Dr. Walker said things about "shock" and "denial" and something about not being able to cope. She acted as if she didn't think I was really sick, but still, I heard her tell Mom and Dad that they should let me stay in bed. Mom asked if they should postpone the funeral until I felt better so I could go! I wasn't going, and I wanted to sit up and tell them that, but I couldn't. I didn't care if they postponed their funeral a million years, I wasn't going. I was going to sleep right now, and even if they carried me into the place where they were going to have their stupid funeral, I would sleep there, too. But then Dr. Walker told them not to postpone anything, to do what they had to do, and then she said something else, very quietly, but still, I heard, and I was really scared. Because now I knew that she knew. She said, "When this is over, maybe Emily should have some help, a professional, not me. I think she's coping with something she hasn't told anyone about."

I wasn't sure just what she meant about help or what kind of professional, but I knew what she meant that I hadn't told anyone about. So she knew, too, then—that it was *all my fault*?

I turned my face to the wall. If I was asleep, they couldn't wake me up. . . .

10

I don't know how long I slept after that, maybe a day, maybe a couple of days. I only know that I kept waking up and it was dark, and then I'd wake up and it was light, and always there was somebody sitting close beside my bed. Usually it was Mom or Daddy, but once it was Millie, and I think one time Dr. Walker came back. Sometimes, when I awoke, it was because Mom or Dad was holding a glass of juice for me, and I'd drink it, and then I'd go to the bathroom, but I was really too tired to stay up for more than a minute.

Once I woke up and Mom was sitting on the side of the bed, shaking me lightly. "Emily?" she said. "Emily, can you wake up now?"

I looked around at the sunlight coming through the

window, and I turned back into the pillow. "Don't want juice," I muttered. "I'm not thirsty."

"Yes, but you have to get up." Mom had a washcloth in her hand, and she began washing my face. It was cold, and I pulled away. "Come on, Emily, you have to get up and get dressed now. Let me help you."

"Why?"

"Because. Come on." Her voice was pleasant, but it was firm, that same kind of voice she uses when I say I'm too sick to go to school, and she says my temperature is normal and I have to get up and go. She made me sit up then and helped me off with my pajamas and into my underwear. I wanted to pull away, to burrow down in the warm bed again, but I had never really refused to do something like that, and I didn't know what would happen. Mom continued to help me, and then she handed me my dress and helped me on with it. It was my green one with the butterfly, the one I wear when I'm going somewhere special. Why? Where was I going? It wasn't a—funeral, was it?

And I lay back down on the bed, and I didn't care what happened, how mad she got, because I wasn't going to do that.

"Are you sick?" Mom said, and she eyed me anxiously, as if she thought I was going to throw up again.

"Yes."

"Going to throw up?"

"No." But I could hear my voice shaking, as if I were about to cry.

"But sick?"

"Uh-huh."

"Well, that's why we're going where we're going," Mom said gently. "We're taking you to a new doctor."

A new doctor? I didn't need that, didn't want it, but it wasn't a funeral.

"Here, let me help you," Mom said, and she put one arm behind my back and helped me up. I sat on the side of the bed for a minute because I was really dizzy, but when I felt better, Mom helped me downstairs. It was quiet in the kitchen, quiet in the whole house. Where was everybody?

Outside, Daddy was standing in the driveway with the car door open, as though he were waiting for us, and when we came out, he came to me and hugged me quickly. But for that second before he hugged me, there was something funny in his face. "How do you feel?" he asked.

Scared, so scared, but I didn't say it out loud, and I shrugged, just barely.

Daddy nodded, as if he didn't expect an answer anyway, and he helped me into the car between him and Mom. He drove, and slowly we went down the drive, past the field, down past Mary Elizabeth's house. And at the bottom, sitting on the wall, strapping on her roller skates, was Mary Elizabeth.

Daddy smiled at her. "Good morning, Mary Elizabeth."

"Hi, Mr. Taylor," she said. She looked in the car window. "Hi, Emily," she said shyly. "Do you feel better?"

I shook my head no, and then I closed my eyes and rested my head back on the seat. How weird, to be out roller skating. I heard Mom sigh, a tired kind of sigh, but she didn't say anything, and Daddy started the car again.

We drove a long way, and I kept my eyes closed, trying to get back to sleep. But when the car stopped, I sat up, surprised. We were in the city, in front of a tall building I had never seen before. There was a long blue canopy outside, and some workmen who were repairing the sidewalk. There was a doorman, too, and when he saw our car stop, he came out to the curb and opened our door.

Mom spoke to him, and he helped Mom and me out, but Daddy stayed in the car. And then, even though I felt weird and weak, when I went in the building, I couldn't help looking around. It was such a fancy place, mirrors on all sides of the lobby, so that as we came in, we could see ourselves walking toward ourselves. Was that me? Boy, was I skinny! Wait till Monse—

Mom and I got into the elevator, and noiselessly it slid us up to the eleventh floor. It stopped, and the doors opened, right into someone's apartment. There was a tiny hall, and more mirrors, and two doors, and before Mom could even knock, one of the doors opened, and a little old man popped out. He was sort of fat, and sort of bald, with fuzzy gray hairs around the edge of his bald spot, but he was tiny, hardly any bigger than I was. He was wearing jeans and sneakers and a plaid shirt, and he looked like any of the boys in the fourth grade. Except that he was an old man!

"Hello, Dr. Weintraub," Mom said.

A doctor! This was the doctor?

Tiny, little Dr. Weintraub shook Mom's hand as if they were old friends, and then he patted her shoulder. "Hello, Mrs. Taylor," he said.

"Dr. Weintraub," Mom said, "this is Emily."

Dr. Weintraub turned to me. "Hello, Emily," he said. His voice was little and friendly, too, but his eyes seemed to run right through me. He held out his hand to me.

I took it, and it was soft, like a child's, and I had this weird feeling that it would break if I didn't hold it very carefully. "Hello," I said, but I didn't look at those eyes.

"I'll leave you two?" Mom said.

"What! No way!" I turned to her and put out my hand, and I almost grabbed her skirt, the way a little kid would do. But then I quickly pulled my hand back and stuck it in my pocket. "Where are you going?"

Mom looked at me and then at Dr. Weintraub, and he looked at me. "She's just going away for an hour or so. We'll just talk awhile, Emily. I don't think you need her here." He paused, then smiled, and it was a nice smile, even though it made him look even more like a little kid. "Unless you want her to stay?" he added.

I hesitated. Why did I feel it would be babyish to say I wanted her? But I did want her, and I couldn't say it, so instead, I said, "What are you going to do to me? Any needles or stuff?"

Dr Weintraub laughed. "I'm not that kind of doctor. We just talk."

"What kind of doctor are you?" I didn't look at him.

"A talking doctor. Some people call us psychiatrists." He laughed softly. "Some people call us other things."

"You won't hurt me?"

"I won't do a thing. You don't even have to talk if you don't want to."

I felt trapped, and I wanted to get away, but they had brought me here for this, so I'd better get it over with. "O-kay," I said slowly. I knew I sounded like a martyr.

Dr. Weintraub laughed lightly. "You won't be sorry," he said.

To myself I said, "Oh, yeah?"

Mom left then so quickly that I knew she was afraid I'd change my mind, and then Dr. Weintraub was leading me down a long hallway and into a big room. He closed the door behind us, and my heart was pounding so hard I knew he must hear it, so that when he pointed to a chair, I sank down, relieved, feeling as if I could hide in that great big chair. I realized suddenly how tired I was, and for a minute I leaned back and closed my eyes. But after a while I felt uncomfortable because I could feel him looking at me, and I opened my eyes.

He was watching me, his little, tiny fingertips pressed together, making a tower out of them. He smiled at me over the tower, a nice smile, but he didn't speak. He seemed to be waiting, and because I didn't know what he was waiting for, I waited, too. We both waited for a very long time.

"I hear you've been sick," he said softly—finally. He sounded sad when he said that, as though he were disappointed that I didn't speak first. "When did you first begin to feel bad?" he continued. "Do you remember?"

Was he kidding? Of course I remembered. It was the day that Monse . . . Careful. He had said I didn't have to talk. But those eyes were pushing behind my forehead again, poking back inside my brain.

"The same day your brother got hurt?" he said quietly.

I looked at him, startled. So he knew about Monse! But he said when Monse got *hurt*. He didn't say *dead*.

He returned my look, nodding just a little, so I nodded, too. "Hmmm," he murmured. "The same day your brother got hurt. That would make anybody sick, wouldn't it?"

I nodded again, harder this time, glad for some reason that he had said that, glad even that he thought so.

"Of course you'd feel sick," he said, still quietly. "Sick and sad, too." And he looked sad himself.

And then I was going to cry, and I wouldn't cry, not here, and I looked around his room. He had shelves piled high with games—checkers, Bonkers, Squash—lots of the same games I have at home. Think about games, not about Monse. Why did he have all those games? Did all psychiatrists play games? Is that what they were supposed to do? Or maybe he wasn't really an old man; maybe he was wearing a wig, one of those skinhead wigs you can get for Halloween. I took a quick look at him.

"What are you thinking?" he said. The eyes were probing me again, but still sadly.

"Nothing. I mean, about your games." I couldn't tell him I was wondering if he was wearing a skinhead wig.

"Do you like any of them?" He leaned forward, and suddenly he wasn't sad anymore.

I eyed the shelf. "I like backgammon."

"I love backgammon!" he said. He stood up, and his eyes were all lit up, and he took a step toward the shelves. "Want to play?"

What a weird doctor! But I was glad to have him stop talking about Monse, even glad to have him looking happy again, so I said, "Sure, I'll play."

"Good!" He smiled, and he rubbed his little hands together, and then he went and got the game and began setting it up. I couldn't help smiling, too. What a funny little doctor—nice, but weird. I wondered what Mom would think if she found out she brought me here so we could play games.

We began playing then, and I found out quickly that I was a lot better at it than he was, but he probably didn't get much practice. I was beating him really badly, but he didn't seem to mind at all, and he kept looking at me and smiling or else making faces at himself when he made a dumb mistake. And he made plenty of those. Then, in the middle of the game, he looked at the big clock on his wall. "Eleven o'clock!" he said. "Your mother will be waiting." He sounded disappointed. "Could you come back tomorrow? We could finish the game."

It would be weird to come back—he was weird—but in a way I liked him. Besides, he looked so hopeful, waiting for me to say yes, that I said, "Okay, I guess so."

He smiled and looked so happy that right away I knew I had said the right thing. We went down the hall together, and Mom was waiting there, and Dr. Weintraub shook hands with her again. "I'm going to see Emily tomorrow," he said. "We have some things to finish."

Mom smiled. "Fine. Same time?"

"Same time," he said.

I hoped she wouldn't ask what it was we had to finish.

11

On our way home that day Daddy stopped at McDonald's, and for the first time in I don't know how long, I felt hungry, starved even. I ordered a hamburger and fries and a chocolate shake, and I ate them all quickly, and then, just as quickly, as we were getting back into the car, I threw them all up. I stood in the parking lot and fought back the nausea and fought back tears that were threatening, and I shouted at Mom and Daddy, who were standing there, helpless-looking, "I told you I was sick! I told you I shouldn't get up!" They took me home and helped me get cleaned up, and I went back to bed.

When they left me alone in my bed and closed the door, I turned over to the pillow, lying still—as though I were dead—waiting for sleep to come. But in its place Monse came, and I could see him in the hospital, wrapped in bandages, and I wondered when he would come back, when Mom and Daddy would come to wake me up, to tell me that he was better, that today was the day he was coming home. Yet part of my brain played tricks on me, and it pretended that he was never coming back, that he had really bled to death, and that it was all my fault. I could see myself in his room, teasing, putting a snake in his bed while he was outside being stung by wasps and crying, and I didn't even know. And then he got up off the lawn, and he came toward me, and he was mad because I had thrown my baseball glove at him, and he started chasing me, but there was blood all over him, and I screamed. The door burst open, and Mom and Daddy both were holding me, and I was sitting up in bed, still screaming. A dream, a nightmare. I lay back down, shaking, afraid now to go back to sleep.

Next day I was relieved almost to get up and go to Dr. Weintraub's office, not that I wanted to talk to him, but more that it felt good to be going there, to be getting away from the house. Daddy didn't go with us this time, and I was pretty sure that he was back at work, but Mom took me and dropped me off in front of the building, and I went up by myself.

Upstairs Dr. Weintraub greeted me at the door just like yesterday, but his eyes probed even harder, as though he had seen something and were wondering about it. In his room, though, everything was the same. The backgammon board was still set up from yesterday, and we got right back into the game. Boy, was he dumb about backgammon! He didn't even seem to know which were safe moves and which weren't, and he kept leaving himself open to my attacks. Sometimes, when I could have wiped some of his pieces from the board, I didn't but made other moves, instead, because I felt sorry for him.

After a while, though, he seemed to catch on, and I noticed that more and more of my pieces were getting wiped out. The harder I tried, the more mistakes I seemed to make, and after a half hour or so he looked at me and smiled. It was that nice funny look that made him seem like a little kid. "I'm winning!" he said, and he sounded surprised.

"I know."

"It's okay." He seemed to feel that he had to reassure me. "You're really a very good player. It's just that you're not paying attention."

"I know, I'm thinking."

"Yeah, about what?"

"About Monse." I'm not exactly sure why I said that, unless maybe I was just testing, to see if he was really listening.

He was, and he was looking at me, too. "What about him, Emily?" He held the game piece in midair, looking at me.

I shook my head. Everything in the room seemed suddenly still, the only sound the clock on the wall, ticking loudly. Sunlight came between the blinds, falling in little stripes on the floor. One of the stripes fell on him, on his hand held over the board. His eyebrows were raised, as though he were still asking that question. "What about Monse?"

I shook my head again. I remembered that day when I had first come here—was it only yesterday? We both had waited a long time without saying anything, and I had waited longer. I could do it again.

He put down the game piece and just watched me.

I looked away and up at the shelves, and it began rushing back at me, the thoughts, about Monse, about dead, about the mower and the wasps, just like yesterday, just like the dream. I was putting a snake in his bed while he was screaming, bleeding. He told me that time he gave me a bloody nose, "People don't bleed to death, dummy." But Daddy said he did.

"What about him?" Very quietly Dr. Weintraub spoke, leaning out of his chair a little, across the board. "What?" It was almost a whisper.

"He got hurt that day."

He nodded.

"It was the lawn mower. They said it ran over him!"

He nodded again, sadly.

"I'm scared."

"What?"

"I'm going to cry."

"That scares you?"

I nodded. "Uh-huh."

"Something will happen if you cry." He said it as a statement, as if he knew.

"Uh-huh."

He didn't ask any more questions, but he looked sad, and I had to tell him what would happen. "I'll cry. Cry and cry, maybe even not be able to stop."

He reached to the table alongside him and handed me a box of tissues. "No!" I said. And then I began to cry, and it was just as I feared—I would never be able to stop. I used up practically the whole box of tissues, and he patted my hand every so often, but eventually, after a while, it wasn't so bad. I put my head back on the chair, and for a long time neither of us said anything, and he didn't seem to expect that I would.

After I had rested for a while, it was time for Mom to come and get me. As we went down the hall together, he kept a hand on my shoulder, and I wasn't quite so scared about the crying or about other things either. But for some reason I didn't want to go home. I wanted to stay here. It was stupid. I couldn't stay here with a weird little doctor! But part of me wanted to, and part of me wanted something else. But what it was, I couldn't tell for sure.

12

Every day for a long time after, I went to see Dr. Weintraub. Mom would take me in and pick me up afterward, and then I'd go home and go back to bed. Now, though, Mom always made me eat something before she'd let me go to sleep, and she sat and talked to me while I did. She seemed sad when I didn't answer her, but I couldn't help it; I couldn't talk.

I couldn't talk to Dr. Weintraub either, but he didn't seem sad, didn't seem to mind at all. Neither of us mentioned again what we had said about Monse that day, and I promised myself that if he ever brought it up or asked anything, I wouldn't answer. Period. But he didn't bring it up, and the only things he asked were about how I was sleeping or how I felt. So most days we played backgammon, or sometimes other games, because that's all either of us cared about, and I knew that he needed somebody to play games with.

One morning, when Mom dropped me off at his office, I had to step around some workmen who were tearing up the sidewalk with big air drills. The drills were noisy, and it was good to get inside in the quiet. Upstairs Dr. Weintraub had the backgammon board set up as usual. We had played this game every day this week, and every day I had beaten him badly. It wasn't that he was that bad at it, but more that he didn't pay attention, but this day I was the one who couldn't pay attention. I lost the first game quickly, and I was losing the second because there was something bothering me. It was a sound, and I couldn't figure it out, and it was making me nervous.

It rumbled, a low, quiet kind of hum, and I kept listening, thinking. What does it sound like? It sounds like—like the mower, our lawn mower! But it couldn't be! My heart was racing wildly, and I had to stop thinking like this. I concentrated, thinking hard what it could be, and then I almost laughed out loud with relief. It wasn't the mower. It was the workmen tearing up the sidewalk, and I could hear their drills all the way up here.

And then I realized how quiet it was in this room. Dr. Weintraub was leaning back in his chair, watching me, very still. I wondered how long I had been sitting like that, trying to figure out the sound, and I felt my face get hot. "I—was just listening," I said.

He nodded.

"A noise. It sounded funny."

He nodded again.

"But it's only the workmen."

"Uh-huh."

"It sounded like . . ." I leaned across the board, picked up the dice, rolled them, and then moved my pieces. But Dr. Weintraub didn't move his, just sat still, looking at me.

"Your turn," I said.

He didn't pick up the dice.

"Aren't you going to play?"

"You said something, Emily, that you thought the sound was what?"

"Nothing, it's your turn!"

"Emily, you're thinking things, lots of things, and you're running away from your thoughts."

"I'm not running away; I'm playing a game. It was your idea to play a stupid game anyway."

He leaned forward and rolled the dice then, and he looked as intent on the game as he had earlier, and I took a deep breath of relief. But then he spoke, and because he was leaning over, he was close and looked right into my eyes. "And because you have thoughts and won't talk about them, you have to keep sleeping. That's why you stay in bed, isn't it, Emily? But it isn't working, is it? The thoughts come anyway." He spoke quietly, and his eyes weren't probing anymore, but they looked clear and very,

very sad, the way I felt inside, as though he were inside me and understood. "It's just not working, is it?" he said again, quietly.

"No." He was right; it wasn't working at all.

"What was the sound?"

"The mower."

He nodded.

"Am I crazy?"

"No, I don't think so, not crazy. It's just memories, and they hurt so much; that's why you're running, why you're sleeping and trying to escape."

"But it was my fault!" I know I screamed it, but it only came out as a whisper.

"Tell me," he said.

"It was the snake." I began to cry. "I was upstairs putting a snake in his bed while he was out mowing the lawn. It was a dead snake, and I didn't do it to be mean, but I was trying to get even with him for teasing me."

"Yes."

"And his room is on the third floor, so if he screamed or called for me when the wasps stung him or the lawn mower ran over him, I didn't hear. Because I was putting a snake at the bottom of his bed where it was all lumpy, and it's *all my fault*."

He was nodding, as though he understood, and he looked sad again, and I put my head back against the chair and cried. I cried until I couldn't cry anymore, and he handed me a box of tissues, and I used them all up and cried some more. But then the crying stopped, and we both sat quietly for a very long time.

After a while Dr. Weintraub said, "Emily, can you explain something to me? Do you mean that if you hadn't put a snake in Matt's bed, then the accident wouldn't have happened?"

"No . . ." I said, feeling confused. "That's not what I meant, is it? It might have happened, but I would have heard him call me."

"Tell me again."

So I told him again, slowly, everything that happened that day, how Monse had let me wear his cap, even about making a sandwich and listening to the mower sounding funny, all the things I hadn't told anybody yet. And when I had finished, he said, "Emily, can we think about some things together? Now suppose—just for a minute—that Matt hadn't decided to do the lawn just then, that he had waited the way he was supposed to, until Millie got there. Then the accident might not have happened, right?"

"It wasn't his fault. You can't blame him; it was an accident."

"I didn't say it was his fault," he said patiently. "I just said it might not have happened, right?"

I shrugged. Maybe, but I didn't see what that had to do with it.

"Okay," he continued. "And suppose that Millie hadn't gone to have her hair done that day, and so she would have been there when it happened. She might have seen something or heard something—"

"But it's not her fault either! You don't under-stand."

But he kept on. "And how about your mom and dad? Suppose your dad hadn't told Matt to do the lawn before his practice? Or suppose your mom had waited for Millie to come that day—she said that she had a feeling she should have waited?"

How did he know all this? Who told him? And what did he mean Mom or Daddy or Millie should have been there? It wasn't their fault; it wasn't any-body's fault! Accidents happen. "It's nobody's fault!" I said. "Accidents happen." And I listened, surprised, to my words hanging there in the air.

There was a long pause while Dr. Weintraub nod-ded agreement, and after a bit he smiled sadly. "Nobody's fault, yet each one takes the blame."

"Mom and Dad and Millie, too?" I said, remem-bering what Daddy had said that day in my room, what Mom had said.

He nodded.

I sat back in my chair. Nobody's fault that Monse was dead. Was he dead? My brother, Monse, he was always teasing me, he had a catch with me, showed me how to play, gave me his hat. And I was afraid. . . .

As if he had read my thoughts, Dr. Weintraub said, "You look terrified."

"I'm scared. I'm scared he's dead!" I cried. "Is he . . . is he dead?"

For a long, long time he just looked at me, and my

heart beat so hard I was sure it would split, would bounce apart like a balloon pushed way past its bursting point. He didn't say yes, and he didn't say no, until finally, he said very quietly, "Emily, you already know the answer to that, don't you?"

I did. I knew it. Monse was dead. I nodded, and he reached over and took both my hands in his because he must have seen what was happening inside me.

13

Going home in the car with Mom that day, I felt different from the way I did other days. Usually I just closed my eyes and pretended to sleep, but today I wasn't able to do that. I kept sneaking looks at Mom. She was thinking about her driving, so I had a chance to study her without her noticing me. She looked better than the last time I had really looked at her, not that old nana look anymore. She was pretty, I thought, for a mother. I mean, she has lots of gray in her hair, but she doesn't look old, and she always dresses so nice, very modern. Today she was wearing tight jeans and a bright pink shirt that I had never seen before. "Where'd you get your shirt?" I asked.

Mom looked at me quickly, seeming surprised that I had spoken to her, and she laughed lightly before she looked back at the road. "This? I bought it a few days ago. I felt as though I needed something bright."

My insides twisted again, as though they were crying, because I knew instantly why she wanted that bright shirt. I swallowed hard to get rid of the lump in my throat, but I guess Mom didn't notice because, after just a tiny pause, she continued. "How are you liking Dr. Weintraub?"

"He's okay, really okay," I answered, but I didn't add any of the important things.

Mom nodded, and she was silent for a long time, as though she were thinking, and when she spoke again, she sounded nervous, in a way I had never heard before. "Mary Elizabeth has been looking for you," she said. "The All-Star game's on Saturday, and she wants to know if you'll play." She looked at me then, a little sad but with her eyebrows raised.

I tried to smile at her to make her feel easier, and I wanted to answer, but there was one thought racing through my head: Three weeks, it had been three weeks since the accident! The All-Stars were in three weeks, Mr. Wallin had said. And the funny thing was, the All-Stars seemed not to matter at all. But Mom was waiting for an answer, so I asked the thing that did matter. "Mom," I said, "where is Monse?"

Mom never took her eyes away from the road, and I had the feeling that for an instant everything about her became perfectly still. I even wondered afterward if her heart had stopped beating for that instant.

"Mom," I said, "I know he's dead. I just want to know where he's buried."

Mom let out a long, slow breath and kept staring ahead at the road. "Emily," she said. "You said you know he's dead?"

"Yes. I guess I've known all along, or at least a part of me has known all along. Where is he buried, Mom?"

"Saint Thomas's," she said quietly. "It's a pretty spot, back by the far stone wall."

"Saint Thomas's?" I couldn't believe it! That's the cemetery across the street from our school. None of the kids ever goes in there, except when we dare one another to do it, because everybody's scared, says it's haunted. Even Monse is always pretending there are ghosts there. And now he was buried there? I just shook my head.

"Emily, are you sure you know, sure you understand?" Mom seemed to have to be reassured like a little kid.

"Yes . . . I do," I said, and I was crying again, and for a minute I wished this was yesterday, that I could go back before today and say that it wasn't so.

Mom looked away from the road then and looked into my face, resting one hand against my cheek, and while she drove, she wiped the tears that kept running there. We drove the rest of the way without saying anything, but it was an okay kind of silence, and I didn't pretend to be asleep anymore.

As we turned into the driveway, I saw Mary Elizabeth in her backyard, throwing a baseball against the garage wall. I wondered if she was practicing for the All-Stars. When I got out of the car, I didn't go right in the house but hung around in the driveway for a minute, half hoping she would come and talk to me, half hoping she wouldn't.

"Emily? Emily?" she called.

I turned and saw her coming slowly up the drive, bouncing the ball up and down in her hand, so casual looking that I knew she was nervous.

"Hi," she said.

"Hi."

We looked at each other, then looked away, and then we both spoke at the same time. "How do you feel?" she said.

"How are you?" I asked, and we both giggled a little, then paused, waiting for the other to speak first.

"Want to play?" she said.

"Play what?"

She shrugged. "I don't know, anything. Have a catch?"

"I guess." Looking at her, I remembered all the things that had happened, how she had acted too grown-up for baseball, too grown-up for secret notebooks, how lonely I had been without her, how I had slapped her that day.

She must have been thinking, too, because she said, "Emily, remember what Mr. Wallin told you about us, that we're a great pair? Well, that's not just for baseball; it's for lots of things. I guess I didn't know how much I would miss you."

"Me, too," I said, and I meant it. But as I stood there, a feeling began to grow inside me, and it was so odd to think how normal everything seemed. We were here in the driveway, talking in the sun, about baseball and the All-Stars, and about being friends, and everything seemed just the same, as though Monse weren't even dead. . . .

"Huh?" She was asking me something, but I hadn't heard, and now she was waiting for my answer.

"Want to play something?" she said.

"Yes, but I have to do something first, okay?"

Her face got stiff, and she flushed a little, and I wondered if she thought I was trying to avoid her. "It's really important," I said. "I promise I'll see you in just a little while."

She nodded.

"See you?" I said.

We were still standing there, looking at each other, when a car came up the drive—Daddy! He stopped and got out and came to us, looking more pleased than I had seen him look in so long. He looked from me to Mary Elizabeth and then to the baseball and back to me again. "Getting ready for some baseball?" he said.

"Yup, some baseball," I answered. "The All-Stars are Saturday."

"We're both going to play, aren't we, Emily?" Mary Elizabeth said.

"Yeah, of course. What a pair!"

Daddy grinned at us. "I'll have a catch with the both of you in a little while if you'd like."

"How about now?" Mary Elizabeth said.

I made a face at her. "I have something to do! I promise I'll be right back." To Daddy, I said, "I have something to do, but as soon as I get back, we'll have a catch, okay?"

Daddy smiled and said, "You bet," and then he went into the house.

I started to follow him, but first I stopped and smiled at Mary Elizabeth. "See you," I said firmly, so she'd know I meant it.

She smiled back. "See you," she said.

14

Inside, I ran upstairs to my room, but for the first time in weeks I didn't climb into bed. Instead, I pulled up all the shades and opened the windows. It was so stuffy. I wondered if Mom had the air conditioner on, but I didn't care; I opened all the windows anyway. Then I knelt down alongside the bed, dug underneath, and pulled out the secret box. I opened it, took out the notebook, but left the hat inside. It was habit that made me look around the room for a new hiding place for the book . . . until I remembered.

With the box under my arm, I started downstairs. It was so quiet in the house, no music, no stereo, no laughing, only two voices talking quietly in the kitchen. Monse always had his stereo blasting in his room, and I realized that I would have to tell Mom that we'd have to bring the stereo down.

In the kitchen Mom and Millie were working at the sink, Millie washing some silver and Mom drying it, and they both turned to me when I came in. It was the first time I had seen Millie since the accident, and she looked so different—older, somehow, and her hair wasn't all fancy, as though she hadn't had it done in weeks. I wondered if it was because of Monse, if she was feeling guilty about not being there, and I wanted to tell her then about what Dr. Weintraub had said that everybody was blaming himself, but it was nobody's fault. I knew someday I'd tell her that, but just now she came to me and threw her arms around me, soapy water and all. She held me tight, and I realized that in all those years, she'd probably never hugged me before, and it felt good. "Emily," she whispered. "I'm so glad."

"Me, too," I said, and I hugged her back before I pulled away. "I have to go," I said to Mom. "I'll be back in a little while. If Mary Elizabeth calls, tell her I'll be right back."

"Where are you going?"

Mom sounded worried, and I busied myself getting out the lock for my bike so I didn't have to look at her. "Somewhere. I won't be long, okay?" I didn't wait for her answer or even look at her again because I had to go away from here alone.

Quickly I went to the garage and got out my bike, put the box in the basket, and zoomed down the driveway. Out of the corner of my eye I could see

Mary Elizabeth still in the yard, throwing the baseball against the garage, but I pretended not to see her so she wouldn't ask either where I was going. But I had a feeling she watched me all the way as I went down the drive until I turned into the street.

It wasn't very far to Saint Thomas's, and I was there in about five minutes. I got off my bike, opened the little gate that stands in the middle of the low wall, and began pushing my bike down the path. So quiet here, some birds, that's all. There were so many graves; how was I going to find Monse's?

Slowly I continued down the path, looking to either side. On one side, big stones, four and five names on each. On the other, small stones, very old, with no names at all, their faces washed clean. How could I ever find his? "It's a pretty spot, back by the far stone wall." I remembered Mom's words and walked more quickly then, to the very end of the path.

There, against the wall, under a deep red maple tree, I saw it. "Matthew," it said on the stone. "Matthew Taylor. Beloved son. Beloved brother."

For a long time I could only look at it. I couldn't believe it, could hardly believe it. I reached out my hand, ran my fingers over the words "Beloved brother." I did love him, used to love him; even when we fought, I loved him. I still loved him. It wasn't fair that he was dead, under the ground, buried, that I'd never see him. It wasn't fair to him that he'd never see anything, never see the trees, the flowers, his baseball team, the All-Stars, or the stupid stone on his grave. Boy, would he laugh if he could see that. "Beloved," he would say, and make a face as if he were going to throw up. "It's just not fair!" I screamed it out loud, and I began to cry. The sound echoed back from the gravestones, but I didn't care, and I didn't think anyone would care. I wondered what Dr. Weintraub would say when I told him, "I'm mad, not sad, *mad*. It's not fair." But I thought he would understand.

After a little bit, though, even the mad feelings began to go away, and I grew quieter inside. I opened the secret box and knelt down in front of his grave. There were flowers in a jar there, red roses, like the creeper roses that grow behind our house, and I wondered if Mom or Dad or Millie had put them there. I took the jar and the flowers and set them inside the open box, then put the whole thing back on his grave again. But the baseball hat was a puzzle, and I wasn't sure what I was going to do with it yet.

I sat down for a while, crying maybe, but I don't know for sure. I only knew that I was here, that Monse was here, buried here, dead, and that I had given him back his secret box. And I knew that I was going to miss him a lot.

I looked at my watch—two o'clock. Daddy was going to have a catch with us, Mary Elizabeth and me, help us get ready for the All-Stars. I stood up, held Monse's baseball hat, twisting it around in my hands, looking at the stains on the inside, sweat, from Monse's wearing it. Did he want it? "Do you?" I asked him out loud, even though I knew it was a stupid thing to do. But maybe it wasn't such a stupid thing to do because I remembered then what he had said that day, that I should wear it. And after all, this was the All-Stars.

I put the hat on my head, picked up my bike, and started down the path to the gate. I knew I'd come back sometime—lots of times—but now I had practice with Daddy and Mary Elizabeth for the All-Stars.

I don't know if I imagined it, maybe it was only a memory, but as I got to the end of the path, I heard it, the same words he had said that day. "Remember," he said . . . and then he smiled at me, and it was his real smile, not the teasing one. "Keep your body in front of the ball."

PATRICIA REILLY GIFF

writes about girls and boys just like you:

• clever • cheerful • stubborn • mad • brainy • average • happy • sad

Show your parents this list of her funny, serious, wonderful books
—to own, read, and treasure for years!

_____ FOURTH GRADE CELEBRITY	42676-6-58	$2.25
_____ GIFT OF THE PIRATE QUEEN	43046-1-00	2.25
_____ THE GIRL WHO KNEW IT ALL	42855-6-51	2.25
_____ HAVE YOU SEEN HYACINTH MACAW?	43450-5-58	1.75
_____ LEFT-HANDED SHORTSTOP	44672-4-17	1.75
_____ LORETTA P. SWEENY, WHERE ARE YOU?	44926-X-11	2.25
_____ THE WINTER WORM BUSINESS	49259-9-25	1.95

Yearling Books

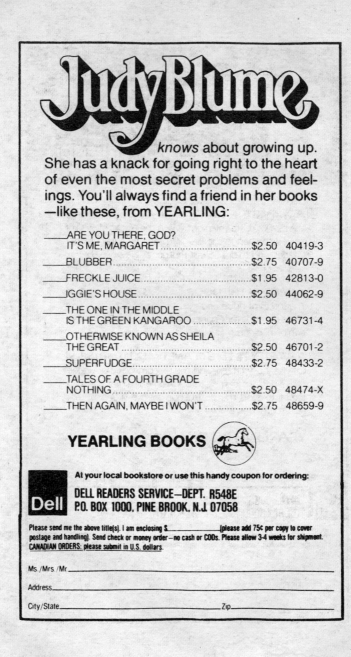